Learning about Water and Energy Conservation

Generously funded by
Riverside Public Utilities

WATER | ENERGY | LIFE

PUBLIC UTILITIES

Little green BOOKS ™

THE ADVENTURES OF A PLASTIC BOTTLE

A STORY ABOUT RECYCLING

BY
ALISON INCHES

ILLUSTRATED BY
PETE WHITEHEAD

LITTLE SIMON

An imprint of Simon & Schuster Children's Publishing Division • New York London Toronto Sydney • 1230 Avenue of the Americas, New York, New York 10020
Copyright © 2009 by Simon & Schuster, Inc. • Illustrations copyright © 2008 by Pete Whitehead • Book design by Leyah Jensen
Manufactured in the United States of America
8 10 9
ISBN-13: 978-1-4169-6788-0 • ISBN-10: 1-4169-6788-5
0413 LAK

JANUARY 1

Dear Diary: Do you ever get the feeling you were MEANT to do something?

Right now I'm a thick, oozing blob of CRUDE OIL
deep underneath the ocean floor, and
I've been here for thousands of years.

But someday I could be made into fuel like gasoline for cars or jets, or I could even be made into tar or asphalt and help build roads.

I hear something cranking and clattering above. I better go check it out!

January 11
Hi, Diary:
Guess what that noise was? It was a huge **DRILL**! I was sucked through a long, wide pipe and into the belly of a giant boat they call a **TANKER** because the inside of the boat is specially designed to carry liquids— like a big, floating fish tank.

Sluuurp!

The ship sailed for more than one week, and when it stopped, I was pumped into an OIL REFINERY. Now I'll be put through machines that will clean me and change me into a form that people can use to make lots of things like gasoline, wax, oil, and, PLASTIC.

I wonder what's going to happen to me next, Diary? WHAT WILL I BECOME?

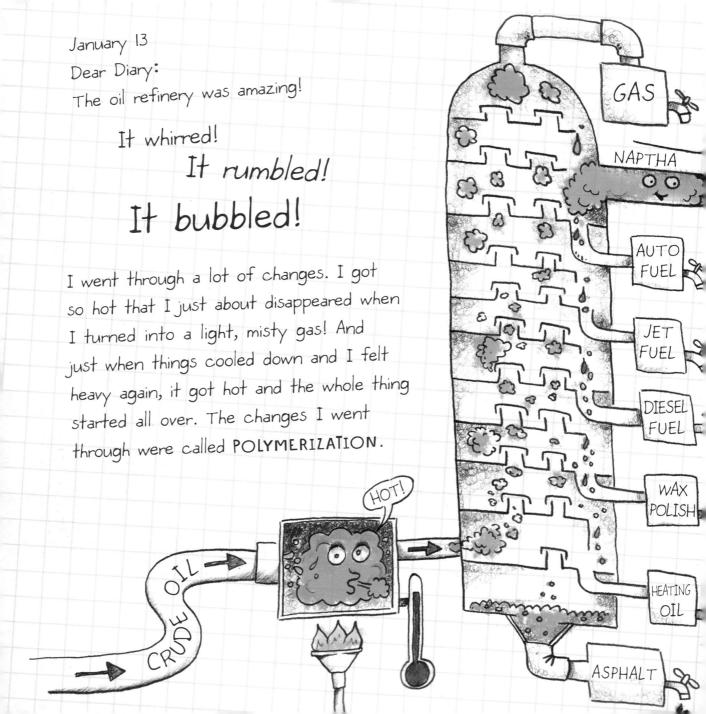

January 13
Dear Diary:
The oil refinery was amazing!

It whirred!
It rumbled!
It bubbled!

I went through a lot of changes. I got so hot that I just about disappeared when I turned into a light, misty gas! And just when things cooled down and I felt heavy again, it got hot and the whole thing started all over. The changes I went through were called POLYMERIZATION.

HOT!

CRUDE OIL

GAS

NAPTHA

AUTO FUEL

JET FUEL

DIESEL FUEL

WAX POLISH

HEATING OIL

ASPHALT

Before I knew it I had become a pile of plastic crumbs! Can you believe it? Plastic! Some of the other crude oil that I traveled with was turned into a paste, some into a thick, clear liquid, and some became a powder. But we have one thing in common—we're all ready to be molded into a new shape.

P.S. Hey, Diary! Did you know that plastic comes from the Greek word *plastikos*? It means easy to mold or shape.

Ah, highly fascinating!

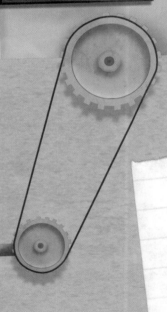

January 29

Hi, Diary:

Guess what? I was sent to a **MANUFACTURING PLANT**, and they heated me until all my little crumbs got nice and squishy. While I was still warm, a machine squeezed me into a mold shaped like a bottle. When I cooled off, I was a beautiful, clear plastic bottle. For REAL!

COWABUNGA!

I felt so light and sturdy as I tumbled into a bin with lots of other bottles. As many as ten million plastic bottles can be made in a day. That's a lot of bottles going out to see the world and never coming back!

Whooooosh!

January 30
Hi-ho, Diary!
Today was so fun! Being a bottle is
great! I was clipped onto a BOTTLING
LINE. Wheeeeee! I flew down the line
and went round and round and up and
down. Along the way I was washed
and STERILIZED. Then I was filled with
fresh water! I even got a spiffy label.

Tee-hee!

They're putting all of us bottles into boxes now. I can hardly wait to see the rest of the world! More adventure awaits me . . .

February 13

Hey, Diary!

Today I arrived at a grocery store. They loaded me into a refrigerator right in the front row where I had a great view of everything around me. The store was filled with plastic containers in all shapes and sizes.

I wonder where we'll all go once we've left the store. . . . Maybe I'll find out soon!

February 14

Guess what, Diary? A boy bought me at the grocery store and took me to a park bench where he gulped down the cool water. The sun sparkled on the side of my bottle. Birds chirped in the tree above me. There were pretty flowers all around. It was so beautiful that I didn't want it to end!

But then something even more wonderful happened! The boy rinsed and filled me with more water, put a flower inside me, and gave me to his mother. I had become a Valentine's Day present! She put me right in the middle of the dinner table. Nothing can be better than being a plastic bottle!

February 21

Dear Diary:

This week was so great, I wish it weren't over! I got to see so many interesting things like the grocery store and the park, and I was a great vase!

The flower wilted and was put into a **MULCH PILE** to become fertilizer. Now I'm in a recycling bin, but I have lots of company— a soda bottle, a peanut butter jar, and an ice-cream container.

February 23
Dear Diary:
After I was picked up by
the recycling truck,

I was brought to a
RECYCLING CENTER
where they sorted all of
the different bottles and
containers.

RECYCLING
CENTER

I landed in a mountain of plastic bottles—now I know where some of those other plastic containers from the store shelves ended up! Did you know we're all different kinds of plastics? You can tell what kind we are by looking at the number on the recycling sign on the bottom of the container.

This afternoon all of us plastic bottles got squished. Then we got stacked in big blocks called BALES and loaded onto trucks.

Here I go again!

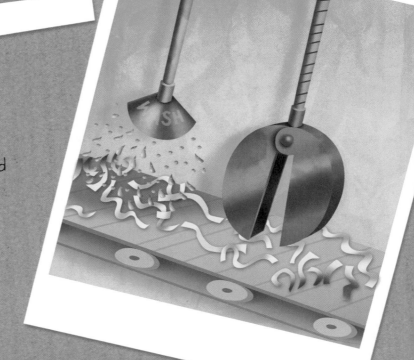

March 16
What a busy day, Diary! I arrived at the plastic reclaiming plant where I'll be made into something brand-new!

I was sent down a line where I got shredded, washed, rinsed, and dried. I'm not a bottle anymore!

Things started to heat up, and pretty
soon I got all soft and mushy.
Then I oozed through an EXTRUDER
where I was squeezed out into
long, thin strands like spaghetti. After
that I got chopped into small bits.
I liked being a bottle, but I think I'm
ready for new adventures!

July 10
Hey there, Diary!
I never thought I could be happier than when I was
plastic bottle, but I am! Can you guess what I am now?

Did you know all of these
things are made with
recycled plastic? Pretty
wild, huh?

Did you guess, Diary? I'm a **SYNTHETIC FLEECE** sweatshirt!
Can you believe something as soft and warm as synthetic fleece
was made from recycled plastic bottles? I went from crude
oil to plastic crumbs, to a plastic bottle, to a vase, and finally
to a recycled fleece sweatshirt. I'm being worn by an astronaut
headed to space.

NEW WORDS FROM THE PLASTIC BOTTLE'S DIARY:

BALE: a large bundle of the same items that are usually tied together

CRUDE OIL: a black liquid found deep in the earth that can be made into gasoline or plastic

DRILL: a machine used to make holes in things

EXTRUDER: a machine that squeezes soft materials to create long strands

MANUFACTURING PLANT: a factory that takes parts and supplies, like plastic crumbs, and turns them into other items that can be sold or used, like plastic bottles

MULCH PILE: an area in the garden where fallen leaves, grass, and plants can be gathered to create fertilizer

OIL REFINERY: a place where crude oil is cleaned and treated to make other substances, like gasoline, wax, and plastic

PLASTIC: an oil-based material that can be molded into items like bags, bottles, and toys

POLYMERIZATION: the changes that happen to crude oil when it's being made into plastic

RECYCLING CENTER: a factory that takes items like plastic bottles, newspapers, and aluminum cans, and turns them into new things that are usable

STERILIZE: to make something extremely clean

SYNTHETIC FLEECE: a type of cloth made from recycled plastics such as water bottles

TANKER: a big ship with a large storage area where things like crude oil can be stored and carried